The
Ice Cream
Store

The Ice Cream Store

poems by
Dennis Lee

pictures by
David McPhail

SCHOLASTIC INC.
New York   Toronto   London
Auckland   Sydney

ISBN 0-590-45862-0

Text copyright © 1991 by Dennis Lee. Illustrations copyright © 1991 by David McPhail. All rights reserved. Published by Scholastic Inc., 555 Broadway, New York, NY 10012 by arrangement with HarperCollins Canada, Ltd.

12 11 10 9 8 7 6 5 4 3 2 1   5 6 7 8 9/9

Printed in the U.S.A.   09

THE ICE CREAM STORE

Oh, the kids around the block are like an
    Ice cream store,
'Cause there's chocolate, and vanilla,
    And there's maple and there's more,

And there's butterscotch and orange—
    Yes, there's flavors by the score;
And the kids around the block are like an
    Ice cream store!

COPS AND ROBBERS

Up and down the fire escape,
Round and round the alley,
The cops ran up,
The robbers ran down—
"STOP!" said Mrs. O'Malley.

GREEN FOR GO

It's red for STOP,
And green for GO—
And catch him all over
Ontario!

SKIPPING (OLGA)

My girl friend's name is Olga,
She's from the River Volga.
She can skip, she can vault, she can somersault—
My acrobatic Olga.

STINKY

My boy friend's name is Stinky,
He comes from cold Helsinki.
He's four foot two, and he smells like glue—
My dinky, slinky Stinky.

DIGGING A HOLE TO AUSTRALIA

We're digging a hole to Australia,
  But it's going kind of slow.
And we've got some juice and cookies
  But they're getting kind of low.

And there's lots of kids in Australia,
  So we brought a sandwich to share;
But if this hole doesn't hurry,
  The sandwich will never get there …

We're digging a hole to Australia,
  Or else to Timbuctoo—
I hope those kids know we're coming,
  And they make us a snack or two!

THE PERFECT PETS

WAL— *I had a DOG*,
     And his name was Doogie,
     And I don't know why
     But he liked to boogie;

     He boogied all night
     He boogied all day
     He boogied in a rude
     Rambunctious way.

SO— *I got a CAT*,
     And her name was Bing,
     And I don't know why
     But she liked to sing;

     She sang up high
     She sang down deep
     She sang like the dickens
     When I tried to sleep.

SO— *I got a FOX*,
     And her name was Knox,
     And I don't know why
     But she liked to box;

     She boxed me out
     She boxed me in
     She boxed me *smack!*
     On my chinny-chin-chin.

SO— *I got a GRIZZLY*,
     And his name was Gus,
     And I don't know why
     But he liked to fuss;

     He fussed in the sun
     He fussed in the rain
     He fussed till he drove me
     Half insane!

NOW— *I don't KNOW,*
      But I've been told
      That some people's pets
      Are good as gold.

      But there's Doogie and there's Bing,
      And there's Knox and Gus,
      And they boogie and they sing
      And they box and fuss;

      So I'm giving them away
      And I'm giving them for free—
      If you want a perfect pet,
      Just call on me.

NINE BLACK CATS

As I went up
To Halifax,
I met a man
With nine black cats.

ONE was tubby,
TWO was thin,
THREE had a pimple
On his chin-chin-chin;

FOUR ate pizza,
FIVE ate lox,
SIX ate the wool
From her long black socks;

SEVEN had a dory,
EIGHT had a car,
And NINE sang a song
On a steel guitar.

So tell me true
When you hear these facts—
How many were going
To Halifax?

THE DANGEROUS TALE OF THE DINOSAURUS DISHES

Oh, the mumosaurus washed,
　　And the dadosaurus dried,
And the kidosaurus took them
　　In her wagon for a ride.

"STOP!" cried the dadosaurus,
　　"STOP!" cried the mum,
And, "STOP!" cried the lady
　　Who was chewing bubble gum.

MAXIE AND THE TAXI

Maxie drove a taxi
With a *beep! beep! beep!*

And he picked up all the people
In a heap, heap, heap.

He took them to the farm
To see the sheep, sheep, sheep—

Then, Maxie and the taxi
Went to sleep, sleep, sleep.

MABEL

Mabel dear
It's not a stable:
Take your front legs
Off the table,

Place your hooves
Upon the floor,
And do not whinny
Any more.

WAITER, DEAR WAITER

Waiter, dear waiter, please come on the run;
Bring me a cheeseburger baked in a bun.

Customer, customer, what can I do?
A mouse stole the cheese, and the burger meat too.

If there's no burger, then bring me the bun.
If there's no bun then my dinner's all done.

HERMAN THE HOOFER

Herman was a hoofer.
　　He hoofed the night away.
He did a fancy two-step
　　On the streets of Mandalay.

He tripped the light fantastic
　　Down by blue Montego Bay.
Then Herman hid his hoofing shoes
　　And slept the livelong day.

COOL PILLOW

Pillow, cool pillow,
Come snuggle with me,
Drift me to sleep
Where I'm longing to be;

Birds in the nest
And the nest in the tree—
So pillow, cool pillow,
Come snuggle with me.

THE VISIT

Saturday night
The moon was bright,
And the Martians began to sing;
And the leader came down
In a calico gown,
Demanding to see the King.

The King was away
Till the end of May.
The Queen had a very bad back.
So the Peppermint Prince
With a packet of mints
Invited them in for a snack.

Saturday night
The moon was bright,
And the Martians began to dance.
Oh, the party was gay
As they gamboled away
In their brand new calico pants.

WE THANK YOU! they cried
As they gamboled outside,
Where the lawn was alight with dew.
(*We thank you!* they whispered
In calico slippers,
As into the darkness they flew ...)

Saturday night
The moon was bright,
And the Martians had flown away.
So the Queen and the Prince
Had the rest of the mints,
And the King came home in May.

A WONDERFUL TRIP IN A ROCKETSHIP

It isn't far to where you are,
    Not if you know the way:
Just zoom around the planet earth—
    It takes about a day.

> *Nantucket, Pawtucket, Biloxi, and Boise,*
> *Manhattan, Milwaukee, and Maine,*
> *Rocketing by in the blink of an eye—*
> *Yosemite, Yonkers, Spokane.*

See how the world spins round and round,
    Like since the world began;
And look—two kids and a spotty dog
    Are racing in Pakistan!

> *Uruguay, Paraguay, Pampas, La Paz,*
> *Panama City, Peru;*
> *Haiti, Havana, and Copacabana—*
> *Quito, Quintana Roo.*

And what do they eat in Bangladesh?
    What do they drink in Rome?
Do kids play tag, or hide and seek,
    In London, Linz, and Nome?

> *Zambia, Gambia, Zongo, the Congo,*
> *Passing like shooting stars—*
> *Maputo and Mali, Zimbabwe, Malawi,*
> *Zambezi and Zanzibar.*

So many faces, so many places,
    So many people to see:
But look, my friend—we're home again,
    And now
            it's time
                    for tea.

CHILLYBONES

Chillybones, chillybones—
Who's got the chillybones?

Rub them, and scrub them,
And warm up their sillybones!

THE SECRET PLACE

There's a place I go, inside myself,
    Where nobody else can be,
And none of my friends can tell it's there—
    Nobody knows but me.

It's hard to explain the way it feels,
    Or even where I go.
It isn't a place in time or space,
    But once I'm there, I *know*.

It's tiny, it's shiny, it can't be seen,
    But it's big as the sky at night …
I try to explain and it hurts my brain,
    But once I'm there, it's *right*.

There's a place I know inside myself,
    And it's neither big nor small,
And whenever I go, it feels as though
    I never left at all.

THE MOUSE THAT LIVES ON THE MOON

The mouse that lives on the moon
Plays the drum with a musical spoon—
    With a laugh like a loon
    He drums, night and noon,
To a musical, mousical tune.

And the cow plays the big bassoon
With her mouth like a macaroon—
    The cow on bassoon,
    While the mouse plays the spoon
In a musical, mousical,
Moo-sical, mouthical tune.

And softly in Saskatoon
A child hears the magical tune:
    The mouse on the moon
    With a silvery *BOOOM*,
    The mooing bassoon
    With a mystical tune,
    And a child who can croon
    To the faraway moon
In a musical, mousical,
Moo-sical, mouthical,
Mythical, mystical tune—
A tune with a moo and a spoon,
The tune of the mouse on the moon!

MY LIFE IN A SHOE

When I was a baby, I thought I was big—
I lived in a running shoe,
And I used to spread my raisin bread
With honey and buttercup dew.

And every day I went out to play
With the bear and the baby raccoon;
And every night, with a bright flashlight,
I swam in the pools of the moon.

Well, now I am three, and I'm big as can be,
And I act like a big kid, too;
But part of me stays in the olden days
When I lived in a running shoe.

I'M NOT COMING OUT

Cover me over
With blankets in bed:
A sheet on my feet
And a quilt on my head,

A frown on my face
And a pout on my snout—
I'm sad, and I'm mad,
And I'm not coming out!

And I don't care if they tickle,
And I don't care if they tease;
I don't care if they beg me to
Until their bottoms freeze,

'Cause it isn't very funny
When a person feels this way,
And it won't be very funny
If a person runs away.

So I'm not coming out, and I'm *not* coming out,
And I'm NOT coming out—and then,
They'll tell me that they're sorry …
And I *might* come out again.

I'M NOT A NAUGHTY DAUGHTER

I'm not a naughty daughter.
I'm not a naughty son.
I'm not a naughty anything—
And now my story's done.

MARY ELLEN MONTAGUE

Mary Ellen Montague,
Won't you come to tea?

Mary Ellen Montague,
Don't you care for me?

If you will not heed my plea,
We must sadly part—

So Mary Ellen Montague,
Please return my heart.

LICKETY-SPLIT

Lickety-split and razzmatazz,
Lickety-split and dandy,
Lickety-split to the corner store
To buy a bag of candy.

One to give a hungry kid,
One to feed my family,
And one to stuff my famous face—
Eating a bag of candy!

ANTELOPE, A CANTALOUPE

Antelope, a cantaloupe,
I can't elope with you;
My poppa wants to come
And my momma does too.

Everybody wants to come,
And tell us what to do—
So antelope, a cantaloupe,
I can't elope with you!

COWARDY, COWARDY CUSTARD

Cowardy, cowardy custard,
Your mouth is made of mustard:
    You talk all day—
    Then you run away,
Cowardy, cowardy custard!

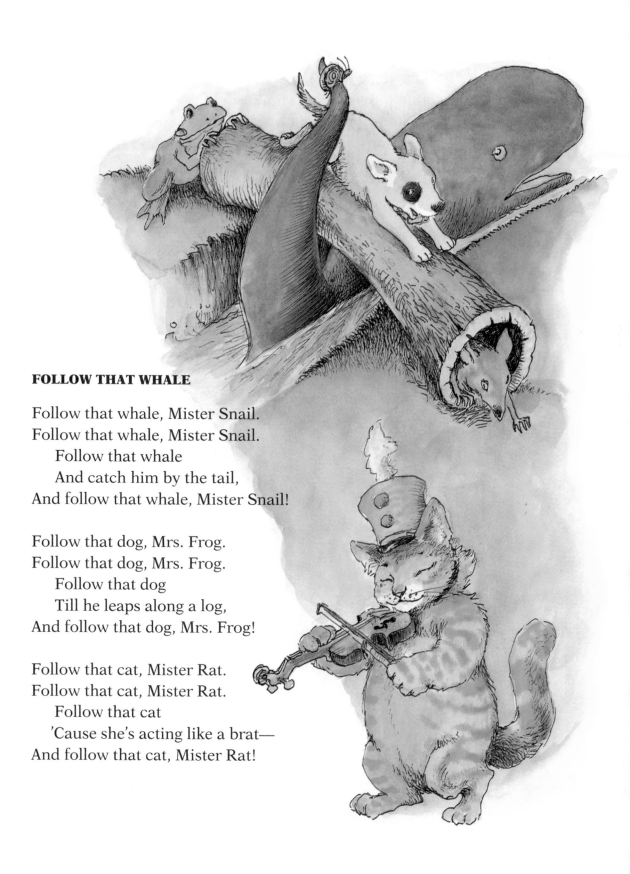

FOLLOW THAT WHALE

Follow that whale, Mister Snail.
Follow that whale, Mister Snail.
 Follow that whale
 And catch him by the tail,
And follow that whale, Mister Snail!

Follow that dog, Mrs. Frog.
Follow that dog, Mrs. Frog.
 Follow that dog
 Till he leaps along a log,
And follow that dog, Mrs. Frog!

Follow that cat, Mister Rat.
Follow that cat, Mister Rat.
 Follow that cat
 'Cause she's acting like a brat—
And follow that cat, Mister Rat!

GUMBO STEW

Momma, don't let me chew that gumbo stew
Momma, don't let me chew that gumbo stew
   'Cause if I chew that gumbo stew
    You know I'm gonna bloat till I block the view—
Please momma, don't let me chew that gumbo stew.

Poppa, don't let me chomp them gumbo fries
Poppa, don't let me chomp them gumbo fries
   'Cause if I chomp them gumbo fries
    You know I'm gonna swell ten times my size—
Now poppa, don't let me chomp them gumbo fries.

Gramma, don't let me taste no gumbo tart
Gramma, don't let me taste no gumbo tart
   'Cause if I taste that gumbo tart
    You know my belly's gonna bust apart—
Gra-gra-gra-gramma, don't let me taste no gumbo tart!

BAPPY EARTHDAY!

There's a tangle in my tungle
   And I can't rock tight,
And I reel so feelie bungled
   That I set I book a light!

But I'm getting all invited,
   'Cause the farty will be pun
Which you graciously excited me
   To come to, sane or run.

So I gapped a little rift,
   Yes I lipped a riddle gaffe …
(When I sing "Bappy Earthday,"
   Don't let Benny Uddy laugh.)

BIG BAD BILLY

Big bad Billy
Had a button on his tum.

Big bad Billy
Said, "I'm gonna have some fun!"

Big bad Billy
Gave a tug, and then a shout—

And big bad Billy
Pulled his belly button out!

DIMPLETON THE SIMPLETON

Dimpleton the simpleton
    Went out to milk a cow.
Dimpleton the simpleton
    Could not remember how.

He pumped the tail, both high and low,
    To make the milk come out;
The cow went MOO, the bucket flew,
    And smacked him on the snout!

QUEEN FOR A DAY

Tina Corinna Christina the Third
Was queen in the land of Tra-La;
   She ruled for a day
   Till they put her away,
For sipping her tea with a straw.

CHICA

My girl friend's name is Chica,
She comes from Costa Rica.
She plays all day, in a very saucy way—
My cheeky Tica Chica.

AKI

My boy friend's name is Aki,
We snack on teriyaki.
With a quiver and a quack when I tickle his back—
My wacky, quacky Aki.

THE KITSILANO KID

Who's that stepping
    Down the street?
It's the Kitsilano Kid
    With the ricky-ticky beat.

Children leave the schoolyard,
    Coppers leave the beat,
For the Kitsilano Kid
    And the ricky-ticky beat.

People know he's near
    By the tickle in their feet—
It's the Kitsilano Kid
    With the ricky-ticky beat, *hey!*
The Kitsilano Kid
    With the ricky-ticky beat!

THE LOTTERY DREAM OF MISS PATRICIA PIG

When I am rich,
I shall live in a ditch.
And I'll wriggle and scratch
Whenever I itch.

SKINNY MARINKA DINKA

Skinny marinka dinka dine,
A puppy met a porcupine.
The puppy barked and ran away—
Skinny marinka dinka day!

CHICKADEE, FLY!

Chickadee, chickadee
Fly away;
Chickadee, chickadee
Do not stay;

Or you will be,
In no time flat,
A chickadee dinner
For a hungry cat!

POLLIWOGS

When polliwogs are paddling
   In the puddles in the park,
Y' know they don't much mind
   If it's light or dark.

They do the wibble-wobble
   As they shimmy in the pool—
Then they flip their little fannies,
   And they swim to school.

CHITTER-CHATTER-CHIPMUNK

Chitter-chatter-chipmunk,
   Fussing on a fence:
All you do is run around
   And get in arguments.

Acorns by the acre full,
   But all you do is scold—
Gather some, and bury some,
   Before the earth is cold.

DING, DONG

DING, DONG,
A short, sad song—
The cat's in a tizzy
'Cause her kittens are gone.

SNICK, SNACK

SNICK, SNACK,
A paddy-whack—
The cat's going crazy
'Cause her kittens came back!

THE BUTTERFLY

Butterfly,
    butterfly,
life's a
    dream;

all that we
    see,
and all that we
    seem,

here for a
    jiffy
and then
    goodbye—

butterfly,
    butterfly,
flutter
    on by.

I KNOW IT'S TIME

I know it's time
To say goodnight.
I know, it's time:
Turn out the light ...

But I loved the one
With the princess proud,
And the one that made us
Laugh out loud;

I loved the one
About the bears,
And that other one,
Where the Daddy cares—

And sometimes I
Could nearly cry,
'Cause I feel so full
And I don't know why

As here on the bed
We ride up high,
And the story goes on,
And the night goes by,

And one day I'll
Be big, I guess,
And I'll have some kids,
And I'll love them best

And I'll tell them the stories
You've told to me.
(But I'll love you still,
And I'll bring you tea ...)

And now it's time:
Turn out the light.
I love you—it's time—
It's time ... *Good night.*

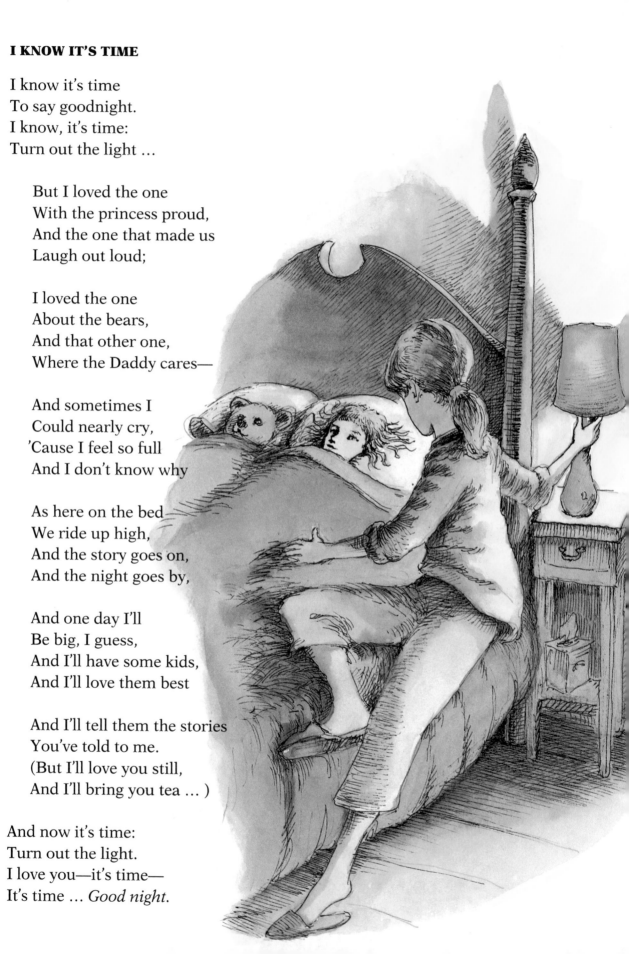

ROSE PETALS PINK

Rose petals pink,
Rose petals red,
Rose petals resting
On your sleepytime head.

(Funny little darling,
Snuggled into bed—
Rose petals dreaming
In your sleepytime head.)

SECRETS

Columbine is sweet
And sweet alyssum blooming—
Tell me who you love,
And I'll whisper what I'm dreaming.

Far as silver stars
In rippled darkness gleaming—
Tell me who you love,
And I'll whisper what I dream of.

Deep as hollow logs,
When phantom frogs are booming—
Tell me who you love,
And I'll whisper what I'm dreaming, dreaming of.

BY THE LIGHT OF THE MOON

The sky tonight
   Is a silvery spray:
It's such strange light
   I'm a world away

As I watch the trees
   And the buildings float
On the rockabye breeze …
   And the moon's a boat,

And the boat slips by
   In a dream of space,
And my heart rides high—
   I love this place!

A HOME LIKE A HICCUP

If I'd been born in a different place,
With a different body, a different face,
And different parents and kids to chase—
　　I might have a home like a hiccup:

　　Like Minsk! or Omsk! or Tomsk! or Bratsk!
　　Like Orsk or Kansk! like Kirsk or Murmansk!
　　Or Lutsk, Irkutsk, Yakutsk, Zadonsk,
　　　　Or even Pskov or Moskva!

But then again, on a different day
I might have been born a world away,
With brand new friends and games to play—
　　And a home like a waterfall whisper:

　　Like Asti, Firenze, Ferrara, Ravenna,
　　Like Rimini, Pisa, Carrara, Siena,
　　Like Napoli, Como, San Marco, San Pietro,
　　　　Or Torre Maggiore, or Roma.

Now, those are places of great renown.
But after I'd studied them up and down,
I chose to be born in my own home town—
　　So the name of *my* place is _____.

GOOF ON THE ROOF

Quick! quick! quickly!
Quiet as a mouse!
   There's a goof
   On the roof,
And he's eating up the house …

Slow, slow, slowly,
Drag him down again.
   There he goes
   Up your nose—
Now he's eating up your brain!

DOOBY, DOOBY

My friend is such a bore,
She bugs me more and more;
She's got this stupid rhyme—
And she does it all the time!

   'Cause she goes,
   Dooby, dooby, in your eye
   Dooby, dooby, punkin pie

   Dooby, dooby, in your hair
   Dooby, dooby, I don't care.

Now, for a little while,
That poem made me smile;
But now it's such a drag,
It makes me want to gag!

   'Cause she goes,
   Dooby, dooby, in your eye
   Dooby, dooby, punkin pie

   Dooby, dooby, in your hair
   Dooby, dooby, I don't care.

Each time I met that kid
I nearly flipped my lid—
Until I got the knack,
And made her stop her yack!

   'Cause I go,
   Dooby, dooby, in your eye
   Dooby, dooby, punkin pie

   Dooby, dooby, in your hair
   Dooby, dooby, I don't care.

LULU

My girl friend's name is Lulu,
She comes from Honolulu.
With an ice cream scoop, and a hula hoop—
My Honolulu Lulu.

JUMBO

My boy friend's name is Jumbo,
He came here from Colombo.
He's big as a house, but he's shy as a mouse—
My gentle giant, Jumbo.

SHAKE-'N'-BAKE A JELLY

If you want a jelly dinner
That's as tasty as can be,
You can shake-'n'-bake a jelly
With a special recipe.

First you bake it in the oven
In a jelly-baking pan;
Then you plop it on your belly
Just as fast as you can;

And your top shakes a little,
And your bottom shakes a lot,
And your middle gives a twiddle
Till your tummy's in a knot;

Then the jelly starts to wibble
On your jelly-belly-pot—
And you've shake-'n'-baked your jelly,
And you serve it, piping hot!

BETTY, BETTY

Betty, Betty,
Cook spaghetti,
Tie it in knots
With pink confetti,

Eat it with ketchup,
Eat it with cheese—
Eat it with gusto
If you please!

POPPING POPCORN

I pop popcorn,
You pop popcorn,
He pops—she pops—
We all pop popcorn!

Pop it in a pot, or
Pop it in a pan;
Pop it in the popper
Like the popcorn man!

HAMMY, THE ESCAPE HAMSTER

I had a little hamster,
And Hammy was his name,
And every time I locked him up
He ran away again.

I put him in a shoe-box,
But I didn't shut the lid;
He ran away that very day
Behind my bed and hid.

So when I caught old Hammykins,
I kept him in my shirt—
But grinning wide, he snuck outside
And woofled in the dirt.

Well then I cornered Hammy,
And I stuck him in a keg.
He took to flight that very night,
And went to Winnipeg.

And then I tried a cupboard
With a special lock and key.
Hammy didn't stick around,
He waltzed to Tennessee.

So then my bright idea was,
To plop him in a kettle.
The hamster hit the road again
For Popocatepetl.

And after that I caught the brat
And wedged him in a drawer—
He made a ladder out of socks
And split for Singapore.

Well, then I tried this iron cage
We bought for our canary.
But with a whoop he flew the coop
And crossed the Kalahari.

So then I put him on a raft,
And launched it in a pool—
The varmint did a cannonball
And swam to Istanbul!

And next a safe, inside a vault,
Inside a ten-ton barrow—
The dirty rascal steered the works
To Rio de Janeiro!

Till finally I sealed him
In a giant gas balloon:
Hammy set the gas alight,
And blasted to the moon!!

But now I've found the answer
And I'm much more satisfied;
Whenever Hammy runs away—
I trot along beside.

THE WATER-GO-ROUND

Oh, the sea makes the clouds,
    And the clouds make the rain,
And the rain rains down
    On the mighty mountain chain;

Then the silver rivers race
    To the green and easy plain—
Where they hurry, flurry, scurry
    Till they reach the sea again,

And the sea makes the clouds,
    And the clouds make the rain …

WILD!

Wild!—wild!—wild!
I am a human child.
The earth was here before we came
And *wild!—wild!—wild!*

Die!—die!—die!
The wild things say goodbye
Each time we take their homes away,
And *die!—die!—die!*

Do!—do!—do!
Before the earth is through,
We have to make it green again—
So *do!—do!—do!*

PETER PING AND PATRICK PONG

When Peter Ping met Patrick Pong
They stared like anything.
For Ping (in fact) looked more like Pong,
While Pong looked more like Ping.

The reason was, a nurse had changed
Their cribs, and got them wrong—
So no one knew, their whole lives through,
That Pong was Ping; Ping, Pong.

THE PIG IN PINK PAJAMAS

A pig in pink pajamas
Went off to the balmy Bahamas—
   Where he sunned at night,
   For fear that the light
Would fade his pink pajamas.

The pig in pink pajamas
Came back from the balmy Bahamas—
   But his skin was bare,
   For the damp night air
Had rotted his pink pajamas!

O pigs in pink pajamas,
Beware of the balmy Bahamas—
   Where the sun's too bright,
   And the tropical night
Will rot your pink pajamas,
   Oh-ho!
It will shrink, it will shrivel
And swinkle and swivel
   And rot your pink pajamas!

DOWN IN PATAGONIA

Down in Patagonia
A walrus caught pneumonia,
From playing its trombonia
While swimming all alonia.

(So when in Patagonia
A walrus on its ownia
Should play the xylophonia,
To guard against pneumonia.)

THE MOTORCYCLE DRIVER

A motorcycle driver drove
    Along a winding road;
He wore a leather jacket,
    And he met a warty toad.

The driver sighed, "I'd like to snooze
    All day beside the road."
"I'd like to drive a big black motor-
    Cycle," cried the toad.

And so the driver settled down
    Beside the winding road.
And off the motorcycle roared,
    Driven by—*the toad!*

FOG LIFTING

In Stewiacke and Mushaboom
I didn't see a thing;
At Musquodoboit Harbour, I could
Hear the foghorn sing;

At Ecum Secum I discovered
Colors in the sea—
And I learned to look at living thing
In Shubenacadie.

THE FIB

I found the fib on Friday
   In a pile of styrofoam.
It looked so cute and cuddly
   I just had to bring it home.
     It was a teeny, tiny fib,
       It's true—
     Till the darn thing grew!

Next morning I was puzzled,
   For the fib was getting fat;
It ate a dozen doughnuts
   And it tried to eat the cat.
     It was a bratty little fib
     So I stuck it in the crib,
       It's true—
     But the darn thing grew!

Next day at five, the fib revived
　　And made a dreadful din:
It shinnied down a sheet it found
　　And kicked the T.V. in.
　　　　It was a healthy, growing fib
　　　　And it didn't like the crib
　　　　So I dressed it in a bib,
　　　　　　It's true—
　　　　But then the darn thing grew!

Well, day by day the fib just lay
　　And slurped its fuzzy fur.
And night by night, in the pale moonlight
　　It munched the furniture.
　　　　It was a whopping giant fib
　　　　And it gobbled up the crib
　　　　And it wouldn't wear a bib
　　　　And its laugh was loud and glib
　　　　　　It's true—
　　　　And still the darn thing grew!

The final morning, when I woke,
　　The fib was in my room.
Its fibby lips began to twitch;
　　I knew I faced my doom.
　　　　Then I was swallowed by the fib,
　　　　Landing on the chewed-up crib,
　　　　Nearly smothered by the bib
　　　　In the laughter loud and glib
　　　　As it roared of Fibbers' Lib,
　　　　　　It's true—
　　　　While on and on, and on and on
　　　　Till the end of time shall dawn—
　　　　　　The darn fib grew!

JENNY THE JUVENILE JUGGLER

Jenny had hoops she could sling in the air
And she brought them along to the Summerhill Fair.
And a man from the carnival sideshow was there,
Who declared that he needed a juggler.

And it's,
Oops! Jenny, whoops! Jenny,
Swing along your hoops, Jenny,
Spin a little pattern as you go;
Because it's
Oops! Jenny's hoops! Jenny,
Sling a loop-the-loop, Jenny,
Whoops! Jenny, oops! Jenny, O!

Well the man was astonished at how the hoops flew,
And he said, "It's amazing what some kids can do!"
And now in the carnival, Act Number Two
Is Jenny the Juvenile Juggler.

And it's,
Oops! Jenny, whoops! Jenny,
Swing along your hoops, Jenny,
Spin a little pattern as you go;
Because it's
Oops! Jenny's hoops! Jenny,
Sling a loop-the-loop, Jenny,
Whoops! Jenny, oops! Jenny, O!

MRS. MITCHELL'S UNDERWEAR

Mrs. Mitchell's underwear
   Is dancing on the line;
Mrs. Mitchell's underwear
   Has never looked so fine.

Mrs. Mitchell hates to dance—
   She says it's not refined,
But Mrs. Mitchell's underwear
   Is prancing on the line.

With a polka-dotted polka
   And a tangled tango too,
Mrs. Mitchell's underwear
   Is like a frilly zoo!

DOH-SI-DOH

Don't be lazy,
    Don't be late—
Jump right over
    The garden gate

Bring your grampa
    Bring your gran
Pile them into
    The old sedan.

And it's one for lights
    And two for luck
As we nearly collide
    With the pick-up truck!

Now here's the fiddler
    Big and fat
Mopping his brow
    With an old felt hat

And here's the caller
    Short and sweet
Trim in the middle
    And quick on her feet

So upsy-daisy
    Don't be lazy
Allemande left
    Till it drives you crazy

Swing with Peter
    Swing with Paul
Swing with the boy
    Who's the best in the hall.

And it's tickle my fancy!
    Tickle my tum!
Tickle my ribs
    Till I beat like a drum!

Now don't be rude
    And don't be rowdy
Tell your lovin'
    Partner "Howdy!"

When he makes
    A bow, by heck,
Grab him round
    His lovin' neck

Swing him quick
    Across the floor—
Pitch him smartly
    Out the door!

And you be candy
    I'll be gum
As we grand-change-all
    Into kingdom come ...

But now the doh-
    Si-dohs are through;
Back in the truck,
    And be
          home ...
               by ...
                    two.

LUCY GO LIGHTLY

Lucy go lightly
    Wherever you go,
Light as a lark
    From your head to your toe;

In slippers you float
    And in sandals you flow—
So Lucy, go lightly
    Wherever you go.

NIGHT SONG

The golden sun
    Has set for good
On every street
    In the neighborhood.

Now through the dark
    And dusky deep
The swallows flutter
    Home to sleep,

And all my friends
    Have snuggled in
To where the sleepy
    Times begin.

Soon other children
    Far away,
From Borneo
    To Bristol Bay,

Will say goodnight
    The way I do,
And dream of far-off
    Places too—

As night comes snuggling
    Soft and curled,
Around the block,
    Around the world.